My Secret Best Friend

WRITTEN BY KIMBERLY ROGERS-BUSBOOM

ILLUSTRATED BY KATI DEE

Dirks
PUBLISHING, LLC

ABOUT THE BOOK

My Secret Best Friend introduces us to Kerri Ann, a young girl on a journey to find a new best friend. Along the way, she encounters several familiar members of the community with whom she interacts, in her own personable way. As the morning progresses into early afternoon, Kerri Ann's heart reveals to her the secret of her best friend. It is, always has been, and always will be, Kerri Ann.

Dirks
PUBLISHING, LLC

Published by Dirks Publishing, LLC
Bartlett, Illinois
www.dirkspublishing.com

Library of Congress Control Number: 2009923667

ISBN 978-0-9823145-2-4

Printed in the United States of America

DEDICATION

My journey to this book is dedicated to all of those who have allowed me the space, the love and the encouragement needed, while discovering my secret best friend. With special love and gratitude to Maury, Brad, Sparky and Pumper...

I love you all.

It was late Friday night.
Yawning and rubbing her eyes,
Kerri Ann cried to her mom,
"I looked all day. I could
not find a new best friend
anywhere!"

She sighed and continued, "Wendy is at her grandmother's. Lizzy is on vacation with her mom and dad. And Elliott has a bad cold."

"Well," said Kerri Ann's mom, "maybe you're not looking in the right places for your new friend."

As she continued to yawn, Kerri Ann replied to her mom, "I am going to get up early in the morning and start looking in new places. I don't want to be lonely anymore!"

Kerri Ann got up early Saturday morning and put on her favorite blue jeans.
She tied pretty pink ribbons in her hair and slipped on her sneakers. Off she
went to search for her new best friend!

Confidently, Kerri Ann walked out the front door.
As she looked up, the rising sun shined brightly in her eyes.

Kerri Ann began to skip toward downtown.
At times, the sun was so bright that she had to
close her eyes to rest them.

As Kerri Ann skipped happily along, she met Ben, the paperboy.

"Hi ya, Ben," said Kerri Ann.

"Hey, Kerri Ann, what are you doing up this early?"

"I am looking for my new best friend. Have you seen her?" asked Kerri Ann.

"Nope," answered Ben. "You're the first person I've seen today."

"OK then, bye!" Kerri Ann replied, matter of factly.

"See ya later, alligator," said Ben.

After Kerri Ann turned to make a funny face at Ben, something caught her eye. She looked back quickly, but there was no one there. "Maybe that was my new best friend, and I missed her!"

As she continued on her way, Kerri Ann saw her neighbor watering her flowers.

"Good morning, Mrs. Livingston. I am looking for my new best friend. Have you seen anyone new around here today?"

"Hello, Kerri Ann," Mrs. Livingston replied. "Why no, I haven't. What does your new friend look like?"

"I'm not sure," said Kerri Ann. But if you see someone, would you please let me know?"

"I will," said Mrs. Livingston.

Kerri Ann waved goodbye. As she waved, she thought
she saw someone again!

"Who's there?" she shouted. Nobody answered.
Now Kerri Ann was getting concerned. She thought
that she had missed her new best friend again!
"Oh well, I guess I'll just keep going."

Finally, Kerri Ann made her way downtown. It was almost lunch time. The sun rose high in the sky.

Officer Kirk was on his horse by the flower shop. "Why hello, Kerri Ann. What brings you downtown today?" asked Officer Kirk.

"I have been looking all morning for my new best friend, and I think I missed her twice now."

"What does she look like?"

"I don't know yet. I think she has been hiding from me all day," said Kerri Ann. "But if you see someone new, will you come and find me, please?"

"I sure will," replied Officer Kirk, as he rode off into the park.

As Kerri Ann waved good-bye, she became very discouraged. "Maybe I scared my friend away," she thought, with butterflies in her tummy. "I'll never find her now!"

Kerri Ann sat down on a bench and put her chin in her hands to think. What would she do now? Her excitement had turned to sadness. Now she was afraid that she might never find a new best friend!

"I have searched everywhere! Maybe I will be lonely forever!"

Kerri Ann stood up and decided to go back home. By now, it was well past lunchtime. The sun was still shining brightly, but it was starting to go down on the opposite side of the sky.

As Kerri Ann started on her way,
a wondrous thing happened...

...she saw her shadow!

Kerri Ann saw the shadow move with her.

She waved at it.

It waved back!

Kerri Ann jumped as high as she could!

It jumped just as high!

Kerri Ann danced with joy! Her shadow danced with joy at the same time.

Kerri Ann shouted with delight. "*I AM NOT ALONE!*"

"*I KNOW WHO MY BEST FRIEND IS NOW!*"

She started to run home as fast as she could. Her sneakers were squeaking, and her pink ribbons and ponytails were bouncing!

As Kerri Ann ran home, she passed Officer Kirk.
She squealed with delight, "I FOUND MY FRIEND!"
Officer Kirk chuckled, and before he could answer,
she was gone.

Kerri Ann passed Mrs. Livingston and her cat Willie.

Kerri Ann yelled, "I DON'T HAVE TO LOOK ANYMORE!
I FOUND HER!"

Willie meowed with glee, and Mrs. Livingston happily smiled.

Kerri Ann was getting close to home when
she saw Ben. She ran past him shouting,
"I FOUND HER, I FOUND HER!"
Ben waved and rode on.

Kerri Ann finally made it home. She ran towards her mother.

"Mommy, MOMMY, MOMMY," cried Kerri Ann,

"THE SUNLIGHT FOUND MY NEW BEST FRIEND!

She has been with me all the time! Now I'll never be lonely again!"

Kerri Ann's mother reached around and hugged her. "How about I fix you some lunch, Sunshine?"

Kerri Ann smiled, rubbed her tummy and nodded. "I think after lunch, my new best friend and I will go out and play!"